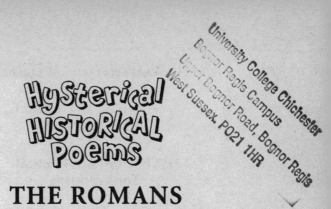

Hysterical HISTORICAL Poems

THE ROMANS

Brian Moses is a poet, editor and percussionist who lives on the Sussex coast with his wife and two daughters. He travels the country presenting his poems in schools and libraries. His knowledge of history is extensive and he can say that almost everything you read in this book might well have been true!

Alan Rowe lives in Surrey with his long-suffering partner and three noisy children where he draws silly pictures for a living. He also plays football, collects toys and refuses to grow up.

Hysterical HISTORICAL Poems

THE ROMANS

Chosen by Brian Moses

Illustrated by Alan Rowe

MACMILLAN CHILDREN'S BOOKS

First published 2000
by Macmillan Children's Books
a division of Macmillan Publishers Ltd
25 Eccleston Place, London SW1W 9NF
Basingstoke and Oxford
www.macmillan.co.uk

Associated companies throughout the world

ISBN 0 330 37716 7

This collection copyright © Brian Moses 2000
Illustrations copyright © Alan Rowe 2000

The right of Brian Moses to be identified as the
author of this book has been asserted by him in accordance
with the Copyright, Designs and Patents Act 1988.

1 3 5 7 9 8 6 4 2

A CIP catalogue record for this book is available from the British Library.

Printed by Mackays of Chatham plc, Chatham, Kent.

Contents

Roman Roads

The Roman roads are straight and neat
One is called Watling Street
It has no corner shops
Or bends
In Dover – it starts
In Chester – it ends

John Coldwell

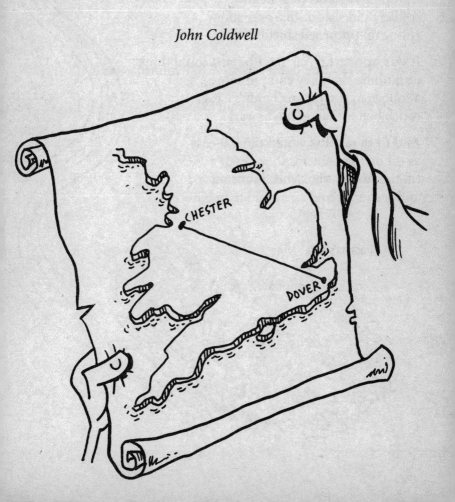

The Vindolanda Run

**(Vindolanda was a busy Roman fort
close to Hadrian's Wall)**

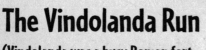

In winter, instead of Roman feet
tramping the iron frost fields,
soldiers slid slalom-like over snow,
riding on upturned shields.

It was wonderful fun, the Romans could think
of nothing that they enjoyed more,
a toboggan run down Cuddy's Crag,
much better than going to war!

And fresh recruits would think it easy
as off on their shields they flew,
till they'd hit a rock and topple off
and the moorland air would turn blue

with Latin oaths and the curses they flung
at an unsympathetic sky –
then they'd dust themselves off and climb back up
to the top for another try.

In the ice and snow it was all systems go
for the soldiers patrolling the wall,
they'd challenge each other to see who could travel
the longest without a fall.

Reputations were made or lost
on a run that went really well.
From around the Empire soldiers would beg
for a post at this once northern hell.

And no one thought of war any more,
Pict bashing had had its day.
The Romans were far too busy
inviting their enemies round to play!

Brian Moses

What Marcus the Guard Did One Snowy Night

I'm the Roman
who built a snowman
smack in the centre of Hadrian's wall.

Ghostly and white,
patrolling the night
keeping us safe from the Scot, Pict and Gaul.

Icy and strong,
it didn't last long
when my Centurion started to rave.

'Marcus you clown,
now just knock it down
or I'll send you home in chains like a slave!'

Decimated, decapitated
wrecked really rotten, really downgraded
bashed, smashed and thumped
totalled and dumped
lost his ears, eyes and nose
in the deep drift of snows
that was the end
of my frozen friend.

But I don't care
because

I'm the Roman
who built a snowman
smack in the centre of Hadrian's wall

so there!

David Harmer

Postcard from Britannia

Mater dear,

        Please send boots,
        hunting nets for swans and thrushes –
        also underpants (it's cold!)
                Your son, Metellus.

P.S. Ma – there is no branch of Marcus et
     Spencerius here! Can you believe
     that?

                    M.

Sue Cowling

Your Empire Needs YOU

Patriots, citizens answer this call
Travel the world, see Britannia, Gaul –
Let your eyes feast upon exotic sights –
Meet foreign natives and duff 'em in fights.

Our fine army offers the best of careers
(To get to the top you'll have 25 years)
Then rest on your laurels in peace and redeem
The pension you've saved in our generous scheme.

We don't allow marriage but think of a life
With no domesticity, trouble and strife,
Just fun with your mates (and the odd little chore
Like drilling in columns and going to war).

It's great in the army AND you get FREE gear –
A sword and a shield and your own high-tech spear,
As well as FREE rations, delicious, piled high,
Free too is your burial if you should die.

We don't mind recruits being not very bright
We just ask you manage a minimum height
Of one point six metres – though ALL SHOULD REPORT.
(We take any stature if tall men are short.)

Small print

In any army you'll get the odd clown –
the coward or waster who'll let the side down,
So just so you're clear and not harbouring doubt
Here are the penalties clearly laid out:

I. Idlers – to wild parts are banished – alone.
II. Deserters or traitors die by whip or stone.
III. Sleepers on watch get to share the pig's trough.
IV. Absconding units get some heads chopped off.*

But let us not dwell on unlikely events
Respond to the offer this notice presents –
Rush to join up and enhance your street cred,
NB. IF YOU DON'T WE MIGHT CHOP OFF YOUR HEAD.

*When caught, one in ten of absconding units will have their heads
chopped off.
That is – the unit will be decimated.

Philip Waddell

Top Five Qualities of a Roman Slave

Ability to be eaten by tigers, but still look as if you're having fun.

Peeling a grape without squirting its juice into your master's eye.

Ability to iron a toga without an iron.

Lying to your master – always telling him that he is the most handsome and powerful master anyone might have when, in fact, he is extraordinarily ugly.

Ability to run very quickly when you do, quite by accident, squirt grape juice into your master's eye.

Andrew Collett

It Could Have Been Reme

Romulus argued
with Remus, his brother
about where to build Rome,
one hill or the other.
Neither gave way.

Bad-tempered, strong-willed,
they fought one another,
and Remus was killed.
Romulus gloated.
'How sad. It would seem
they'll be calling it Rome.
But it could have been Reme!'

Marian Swinger

Woad

(All the Britons dye their bodies with woad, which produces a blue colour, and this gives them a more terrifying appearance in battle... Caesar.)

Let's all go out
and plaster ourselves with woad
(yeah woad!)
frighten everybody silly
as we stomp down the Roman road
(in woad!)

Once we've covered ourselves
with woad,
we'll look twice as ugly
as a warty toad
in woad
(yeah woad!)

We're walking down the Roman road
wearing woad.
Walking down the Roman Road
wearing woad.

Woad is great
woad is cool.
Woad will defeat
the Roman rule.

Woad will help us all
to survive
rushing chariot queues
on the M XXV.

We're walking down the Roman road,
wearing woad
Walking down the Roman road
wearing woad.

Saw ourselves in the lake
and nearly died,
you haven't lived
if you haven't tried
'WOAD!'
(yeah woad)

The fashion accessory
of the Iron Age

Brian Moses

Caesar, (Gaius) Julius (100–44BC)

People born in times BC
Leave me in a sort of fix –
Take Caesar's dates – it seems to me
He died aged *minus* 56!

Philip Waddell

How to Count in Roman

Eye.
Aye-aye.
Aye-aye, eye.
Ivy.
Vee.
Vee eye.
Vee aye-aye.
Vee aye-aye, eye.
Eye eggs.
Eggs.

Nick Toczek

Foot-Soldier's Song

My breastplate's gone rusty – it creaks.
There are cracks in my helmet – it leaks.
This island is cold, wet, and too far from home.
shall I ever again see Rome?

We all hate the natives that lurk in the trees,
and the blustery gales and the rivers that freeze
but the thing that is driving us nearly insane
is the rain.

Our sandals were made of strong leather
but they're no good at all in this weather.
Our shoestrings are rotted, but on we must plod
day after day through the slippery mud.

We're told we must stay, settle down in this land,
but that's the last future I'd ever have planned.
I long to see Rome and its sunshine again
but our fate must be Britain and rain, rain, rain . . .

Pamela Gillilan

The Roman Arena

Send in the heroes with helmet and blade
Proud executioners, worshipped and paid.
Bring on the captive, the Christian, the slave,
Who will beg mercy and who will be brave?

The Emperor's smile
Is as cold as a knife.
Thumbs down for death,
Thumbs up for life.

Lead in the beasts with their swift, silver claws,
Stalking their victims with blood-hungry jaws.
Jeer at the cowards who shiver with fear,
Cheer for the villains who fight with a sneer.

The Emperor rises,
The crowd holds its breath.
Thumbs up for life,
Thumbs down for death.

Clare Bevan

Cowardi Custardus

I'm Cowardi Custardus
A small gladiator
My opponent is massive
I'm off, see you later.

Richard Caley

The Romans in Britain

(A history in under 40 words)

The Romans gave us aqueducts,
fine buildings and straight roads,
where all those Roman legionaries
marched with heavy loads.

They gave us central heating,
good laws, a peaceful home . . .
then after just four centuries
they shuffled back to Rome.

Judith Nicholls

Defixio (or 'I'll Fix You!')

SUIRAM
(The centurion who nicked my best cloak)

May your legion be sent to Britain
Where the rain never stops
May your feet rot
May your bones be shot
With pain like fire
May you drown in the mire
Sink down into Hades
Expire –
    You dog!

PHRIX – PHRAX – PHROX

Patricia Leighton

Defixio – a curse (with the name written backwards and magic words at the end!) The Romans wrote them on small tablets and nailed them on tombs or threw them into sacred wells or springs. Hundreds and hundreds have been found!

Boudicca

Boudicca, or Boadicea,
Was a Queen with one idea –
Fight the Romans, send them packing,
Serve them right for their attacking.

In her chariot she rode
Dressed in style and streaked with woad,
No one braver, no one fleeter,
Till the Romans went and beat her.

Boudicca, with red hair flying,
Drank some poison and lay dying,
Yet although her luck was rotten,
She has never been forgotten.

Clare Bevan

Boadicea

When Boadicea was on the road,
She didn't heed the Highway Code,
And if she met a Roman crew,
Cried, 'Fancy running into you!'

Colin West

On Your Mark . . .

'Friends, Romans, Countrymen –
        lend me your ears,'
Mark Antony once pleaded.
'Not likely!' came the swift reply,
'*We* bring along what's needed,
But *you're* always forgetting things!
(You still haven't returned Cicero's spare toga . . .)'

Trevor Harvey

Recipe for Garum
(A favourite Roman sauce)

Rotting fish skins six weeks old,
Heads, guts and tails growing mould,
Marinate long in a pot of brine,
Then serve it up – it's just divine!

Anne Logan

What's for Cena?

The Romans had a varied diet
I wonder if you'd like to try it?

Let's start with a simple dish
of broccoli baked with rotten fish.
Now try dormice stuffed with pork,
a peacock brain, a roasted stork,
fat milk-fed snails, frogs in mustard,
boiled ox-tails, nettles in custard,
flamingo tongues fried with tomatoes:

I'm sure you'll like a lot of those.
Some crow and cabbage; lumps of horse,
jellied snake in seaweed sauce,
jackdaws, thrushes, stewed cow's udder –
why have you begun to shudder?
If you had too much and your tummy's sore
the vomitarium's through that door.
Do what the Romans did – be sick
and then come back for more. Be quick!

Dave Calder

Julius Caesar's Little-Known Family

Julius Sneezer suffered from asthma
As did Julius Wheezer.
Parmesan was a favourite snack
For the hungry Julius Cheeser.

Julius Breezer had a problem with wind
While Julius Freezer was cold.
Everyone fell for the jokes and tricks
that Julius Teaser told.

Bad-tempered Julius Geyser
Blew his top every day.
Julius Visa travelled the world
Julius Pisa leant one way.

The tenth of the brothers was very polite
Being Julius Pleaser
These are the little-known brothers
Of the famous Julius Caesar.

But they treated the sister with great respect,
Just like the Mona Lisa
She was the Roman wrestling champion
Enter . . . Julia Squeezer!

Paul Cookson

The Advice Julius Caesar Ignored

Your personal horoscope for March 15th

Be sure to spend the day at home – you've more than
Earned a rest from the tiresome duties of State.
Write that long overdue memorandum banning
All cutlery, especially sharp knives, from the Senate
Restaurant. The 15th is a very auspicious day in which to
Enjoy domestic activities or hobbies. I suggest

The following as being especially well starred.
Have a stab at that challenging jigsaw of the forum.
Earmark the day to start lyre lessons.

Invite amusing guests to lunch – NOT republican
      senators and
DON'T, on any account, invite Marcus Junius Brutus.
Entertain your friend Cleopatra. If Cleo's busy try
Spending the day with your wife. Then again you might

Organise the laying out of the new herb garden or just
Find a shady spot in which to relax and quietly

Meditate before your next round of battles.
Alternatively attacking your huge pile of fan mail or
Reading a light blockbuster scroll or even
Cleaning the chariot – would all make for a pleasant day.
Heed this though – whatever you do DON'T GO TO THE
SENATE!

Your soothsayer

Philip Waddell

The Caractacus Chariot Company

FOR SALE:
SECOND-HAND WAR CHARIOT

One Careful Owner (rumoured to be
Queen Boudicca of the Iceni)
Low Mileage
Two or Four Horsepower
Wheels with Sharp Knives (if required)
5 months Woad Tax
Blood-Red Bodywork
inlaid with Roman Bones

Has taken part in several
Successful Battles:
       the Sacking of Camulodunum
       Attacks on Londinium
       Many Minor Skirmishes

Backed by our First Class Druid Warranty

Must be seen to be believed!
Only 3 gold pieces o.n.o.

Will Exchange for quantity
of belts, buckles and bronze shields.

Don't delay, view today, at

The Caractacus Chariot Company™

Mike Johnson

Big Plans for a Big Empire

Bodjitea, the Chief Builder
stuck his pencil behind his ear,
Whistled through his teeth
then tut tut tutted
as he stood in front of the Emperor and Master Architect.

'It'll cost you, this lot,' he said
while shaking his head at the plans.
'It's not cheap, *and* it'll be a long job,
all these fancy buildings and temples and things,
not to mention those straight roads and the drains.
Plus the baths are a bit ornate too.
Take some time they will.
'Course, I'll need labour costs,
time and a half for the lads at weekends
and double time on any holy days or feast days.'

'You want it finished when?
You'll be lucky!
Rome wasn't built in a day you know.'

Paul Cookson

Equus*

The Emperor Caligula
Was mad, of course.
To help him rule
He promoted to the Senate
His horse

The horse was good and just
But rather negative they say
In big debates
The horse would always answer
Neigh!

*Latin for Horse

Roger Stevens

Roman Baths

Have a hot bath, a hot bath relaxes.
  Who cares if you can't afford to pay taxes?
  Who cares if your slaves start to riot and revolt?
  Who cares if you've run out of spices or salt?

Have a hot bath, a hot bath revives.
  Who cares if brown bears have eaten your hives
  and you can't sell your honey around the town?
  Who cares if the Emperor gives you 'thumbs down'?

Have a hot bath, a hot bath is best.
  Here's Pompeian pumice and perfume – just rest.
  Who cares if barbarians disturb the *pax*?
  Have a hot bath. Relax.

Mike Johnson

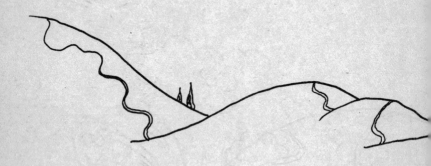

A Quick Roman Limerick:

A Roman is always a Roman
Wherever he's marching or roamin'
Whether out in hot Syria
Or down in Illyria
He's a pigeon who'd like to be homin'.

Trevor Millum

Hadrian's Wall

When they finished Hadrian's Wall
The Romans gave a shout
'Oi! You terrible Picts and Scots!
We've built a wall to keep you out!'

But the Picts and Scots only laughed
And answered with a grin
'Thanks for doing all the work
We've now got a wall to keep you in!'

Marcus Moore

Some Sum

Doing Roman sums is hard,
As hard as hard can be.
I've only just discovered
That L plus L make C.

John Kitching